TEEN TITANS™
Can't Take a Joke

Written by Acton Figuera
Illustrated by Craig Rousseau,
with color by Lee Loughridge

Published by Scholastic Inc. SCHOLASTIC and associated logos are trademarks and/or registered trademarks of Scholastic Inc.

ISBN 0-439-75476-3
Designed by Henry Ng

12 11 10 9 8 7 6 5 4 3 2 1   5 6 7 8 9 10/0

Printed in the U.S.A.

First printing, November 2005

SCHOLASTIC INC.

| New York | Toronto | London | Auckland | Sydney |
| Mexico City | New Delhi | Hong Kong | Buenos Aires |

A man walked into a bank. He waited in line like everybody else. When he reached the teller, he smiled and asked, "Why couldn't the sneakers go out and play?"

The teller rolled her eyes. "I don't know," she replied. "Why couldn't the sneakers go out and play?"

The man chuckled. "Because they were *all tied up!*"

"Very funny," said the teller, not meaning it. She reached for her pen, but her arm wouldn't budge. She was tied up! Everyone else in the bank had been wrapped up with shoelaces, too.

"Nobody move!" said the man. He laughed. "Oh, right—you can't! I'm the Punster, and this is a robbery!"

The Punster stepped over the security guard near the safe. "When is a door not a door?" he asked.

"I don't know—when?" the security guard replied.

When it's ajar!" the Punster shouted. The big safe swung open slightly. The Punster grabbed bags of money and walked out of the bank.

The next morning, the Teen Titans discussed the robbery. "So this guy tells a bad joke and suddenly everyone in the bank is tied up," said Robin. "The punch lines of his jokes come true . . . like magic!"

"That never happens when *I* tell a joke," said Beast Boy.

"Every time *you* tell a joke, I magically fall asleep," Raven said.

"Very funny!" said Beast Boy. "Now what are we going to do about the Punster?"

The Teen Titans decided to each watch a different bank.

In the form of a spider, Beast Boy hung on a long thread above the tellers in a busy bank. As each person spoke to a teller, Beast Boy listened for jokes.

Finally, after a long, boring wait, he heard a man ask, "What did the tie say to the neck?"

The teller had been warned to watch out for the Punster, but she loved jokes. "I don't know," she said. "What *did* the tie say to the neck?"
"I think I'll just hang around for a while!" replied the Punster.

The teller started to laugh, but then she realized that she—and everyone else in the bank—was suddenly stuck in sticky webs. "I know you!" the teller cried. "You're the Punster!"

"Right you are," said the Punster. "I'm punny and I love money." He quickly broke open the safe and entered it.

Meanwhile, Beast Boy struggled to break free of the sticky web. How embarrassing, he thought. I'm a spider caught in a web!

Beast Boy turned into a fat walrus and crashed to the ground, free of the web. Then, as a snake, he slithered silently over to the safe.

The Punster was still inside, filling his bags with money. Beast Boy transformed into a gorilla and sprang forward to slam the safe door shut with the Punster inside.

The Punster slipped out of the safe just in time. "You almost got me, Beast Boy," he said. "Tell me something. What do you say when a dog runs away?"

"I don't know," Beast Boy replied without thinking. "What *do* you say when a dog runs away?"

"*Dog-gone!*" said the Punster.
As Beast Boy tried to grab the villain,
he disappeared in a puff of smoke!

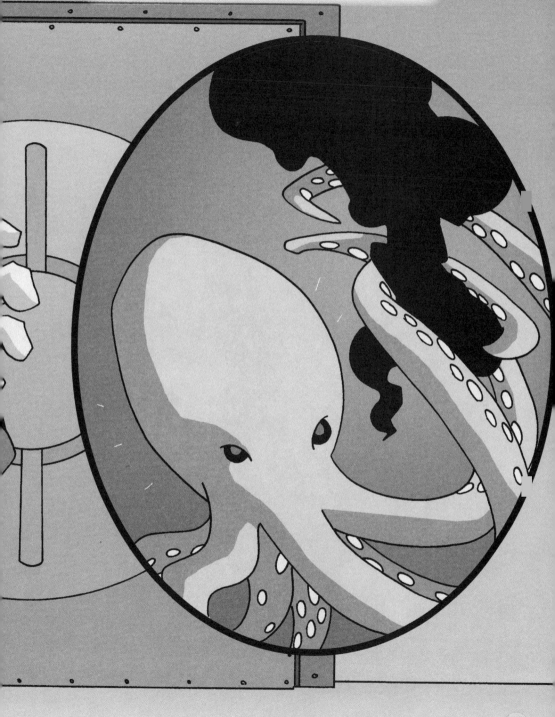

Back at Titans Tower, Beast Boy told his teammates what had happened.

Robin said, "You tried to stop him, but the Punster's jokes are too hard to resist."

"I think the Punster's jokes are even worse than yours, Beast Boy," said Raven.

I don't know, thought Beast Boy. Some of his jokes sounded kind of funny.

"The question is: Where will the Punster strike next?" said Raven.

"Both banks were in the same neighborhood," said Starfire. "Is there another bank close to those two?"

"There's a bank three blocks from here," said Cyborg. "That's the closest one to the two other crime scenes."

"Teen Titans, go!" shouted Robin.

Inside the bank, the Teen Titans spread out and tried to blend in. Before long, the Punster entered the bank and got in line.

The Titans closed in on him.

When it was his turn, the Punster asked the teller, "What did the stamp say to the envelope?"

This teller was hard of hearing. "What did you say?" he asked. "Speak up!"

"What did the stamp say to the envelope?" the Punster repeated.

"You should have filled out a deposit envelope before you got in line," said the teller grouchily.

The Teen Titans got ready to pounce.

"Okay, okay!" cried the Punster. "The stamp said, *I'm stuck on you!*"

Instantly the Punster's magic made everyone in the bank sticky like glue. People's feet stuck to the floor. Their arms stuck to their sides. The teller's hands bonded to her pen and to her desk.

"I am the Punster, and this is a stickup! Get it? Ha-ha!"

As the Punster opened the safe, Beast Boy shape-shifted to escape the glue. He turned into a porcupine, a seal, an otter, and a sea cucumber, but he was still stuck in all those shapes.

Finally, he changed into a giant slug. By sliding on his own slippery slime trail, he slowly oozed toward the safe.

The Punster stepped out of the safe. "Are you looking for me, Beast Boy?" he asked. "Quick, what do you call a crab that plays baseball? *A pinch hitter!*"

Beast Boy turned into a crab and soared across the bank like a baseball knocked into left field.

"Are you ready to give up, Beast Boy?" the Punster asked. "Or would you like one more joke just for fun?"

Beast Boy lay on the floor, gathering his strength.

"What do cows give each other when they meet?" the Punster asked. He loved this joke so much that he giggled as he thought of the punch line.

Beast Boy sat up. *"A milkshake!"* he shouted. "When cows meet they give each other a milkshake!" He jumped to his feet.

"Uh-oh," said the Punster. "Um . . . what part of the body can you put in a sandwich?"

"Easy!" shouted Beast Boy. *"Below-knee!"*

No one had ever beaten the Punster to the punch lines of his own jokes before. If he didn't say the punch line, there was no magic. He tried to think of a good joke that Beast Boy wouldn't have heard before.

"I've got one!" the Punster cried. "Why was the picture sent to jail?"
"*It was framed!*" yelled Beast Boy.

"Why was the teacher cross-eyed?" the Punster asked nervously. Behind him, Starfire had freed herself from the gluey mess.

Beast Boy shouted, *"Because he couldn't control his pupils!"*

Starfire zapped the Punster and knocked him out cold. Everyone in the bank became unstuck. Robin, Raven, and Cyborg rushed over. Robin peered down at the Punster, who was snoring loudly. "Nice shot, Starfire," he said. "Good work, Beast Boy."

"I'm surprised your jokes can be used for good instead of evil," added Raven.

"Thanks!" said Beast Boy. "Say, what do robbers eat as a snack?"

None of the other Teen Titans knew.

"Milk and crookies!" said Beast Boy with a laugh.